Ruby Rogers
Party Pooper

Sue Limb

Illustrations by Bernice Lum

BLOOMSBURY

First published in Great Britain in 2008 by Bloomsbury Publishing Plc
36 Soho Square, London, WID 3QY

A CIP catalogue record of this book is available from the British Library

ISBN 978 0 7475 9247 1

All papers used by Bloomsbury Publishing are natural, recyclable
products made from wood grown in well-managed forests.
The manufacturing processes conform to the environmental
regulations of the country of origin.

Printed in Great Britain by Clays Ltd, St Ives Plc

1 3 5 7 9 10 8 6 4 2

www.suelimb.com
www.bloomsbury.com

CHAPTER 1
Ruby! Stop it!

T HEY CORNERED me at break. I knew
Yasmin had something on her mind because
she hadn't been as giggly as usual. In fact, when I'd
come back from the loo in the middle of history,
I'd seen her whispering with Hannah. They were
cooking up something.

I'd tried to avoid them by imagining I was a
monkey (what else?) and swinging along the fence
at the edge of the schoolyard. I did a few monkey
hoots, scratched my head and beat my chest like a
gorilla. But a whole gang of chimpanzees – real

ones – couldn't put Yasmin off once she gets an idea in her head.

'Ruby! Listen!' She and Hannah came running up just as I reached the far corner of the fence, by the recycling bins. 'We've had a brilliant idea!'

'OOoooh – oh-oh-oh-oh-oh-oh!' I cried, sticking out my lower lip and examining my fleas.

'Ruby! Stop it a minute!' Yasmin's eyes flared slightly. Her eyebrows plunged down towards her nose in a stressy frown. I couldn't ignore these warning signs. Yasmin was going to get in a strop if I didn't stop monkeying around.

'OK,' I said, transforming myself instantly into a gangster instead. 'Whassup? Give me da low-down, Big Yas.'

'I am *so* not big!' snapped Yasmin.

'Sorry,' I said. 'Diamond Lil, then.'

'Never mind all that gangster stuff!' said Yasmin. 'Just listen to our idea! We could have a sleepover on Midsummer's Night! We could cele-brate with bonfires and singing and dancing and stuff to drive away the evil spirits! And we could sit up all night and watch the sun come up!'

We've been doing the Celts in history and I think Yasmin had got a bit carried away with it all. I knew it would be a mistake to argue.

'OK,' I said. 'Count me in.'

'Of course we're counting you in, Ruby!' Yasmin grinned. 'Because the sleepover's going to be at your house!'

'Yes!' said Hannah. 'I've never slept up in your tree house. Oh please, Ruby! It'll be brilliant!'

A sick feeling spread through my tum. My tree house is special. Not everybody climbs a rope ladder every time they go to bed. There's room up there for one, maybe two, but three would be too much of a squash. I didn't want Hannah up there. I knew she would flick her long hair about and make my eyes sting.

'I'd really love to,' I lied, 'but my mum will say no.'

'No, she won't!' yelled Yasmin. She was in a wild mood. Maybe an evil spirit was already egging her on. 'Your mum's lovely! She'll say yes! She won't mind!'

'Midsummer's Day is at the weekend,' said Hannah, 'so everyone can have a lie in next morning. And we won't make a noise or anything.'

'So we're going to have bonfires and singing and dancing in total silence, then?' I asked in a sarcastic voice.

'Ruby! Stop it!' snapped Yasmin. 'Anyway, it's

your turn to have a sleepover! I've had a sleepover, Hannah's had a sleepover, Froggo had a sleepover at Hallowe'en – now it's your turn.'

'But you stayed at my place last week,' I argued feebly.

'That wasn't a sleepover!' hissed Yasmin. 'A sleepover is a party, right? With loads of people and games and stuff.' I could just imagine what Mum's face would look like when I mentioned all this. She would turn to stone.

Basically, Mum's always tired and sensible. It's not what you'd call a brilliant combination. She's out delivering babies all day, so when she comes home she's shattered. Also, she hates all that evil spirits stuff. How were we going to smuggle an all-singing, all-dancing, bonfire-burning, evil-spirit-scaring Midsummer's Night of Celtic Madness past her? We were hardly going to be able to disguise it as a Fairies and Princesses Makeover Party.

'OK, I'll ask her,' I said. I couldn't get out of it. They were right, it was my turn. I'd enjoyed brilliant sleepovers at Yasmin's and Hannah's and Froggo's and Lauren's.

'Great,' said Yasmin. 'We should invite Froggo and Max, and Alice and Emily and Grace and Danny and Charlie.'

'And Lauren,' I said. 'That was a great sleepover at Lauren's.' Lauren lives on a farm and we'd had a whole attic to ourselves, and Lauren's mum and dad didn't mind how much noise we made because they were far away in another part of the house.

'Where is Lauren today?' said Yasmin. 'I hope she hasn't got chicken pox – or duck pox!' She laughed.

'Or mad cow disease!' Hannah giggled.

'Or pig flu!' Yasmin did a kind of cough that was a bit like a pig snorting, and she and Hannah laughed so hard they almost choked. I smiled, but

9

I wasn't quite so amused. There's always a little bit of tension between Yasmin and Lauren. They get on fine, really, but I think Yasmin's jealous, sometimes, because I love going to Lauren's farm so much.

Just then the bell rang, so we had to go back to our classroom. Yasmin and Hannah were making noises of ill animals: a lion with a sore throat, a cockerel being sick, that sort of thing. I suppose it was funny, but I wasn't really in the mood.

I love sleepovers in other people's houses, but it's different when you're in charge of everything. Would my mum and dad say yes in the first place? And if they did, where could everybody sleep? Already I was in a stress about it, and the idea was only five minutes old. I wasn't looking forward to going home tonight and breaking the dreadful news. I knew my mum would go mental.

CHAPTER 2
Don't drag me into it

I HURRIED HOME in a total stress. Mum had to say yes. If she said no, I was dead meat. Yasmin would never speak to me again. Froggo would never pull faces at me again. I would be totally blanked by everybody. I would be nowhere, nobody, nothing.

'Mum!' I burst into the kitchen and threw my schoolbag in the corner. Mum, who had been unpacking some groceries, looked a bit surprised. She didn't look cross, though. Not yet.

'Mum, listen . . .' I hesitated. I had to be clever

now. No use just blurting it out. That wouldn't be smart. I knew what I had to do – make it sound educational. 'We had the most amazing lesson today in school!'

'Oh, lovely, pet. What was all that about, then?'

'It was about the Celts! That old tribe! We're Celts, aren't we – because you come from Wales!'

Mum thought for a split second, and then nodded. 'Well, yes, I suppose we are, Ruby. That's nice, isn't it?' She turned back to her unpacking.

Wait! I thought. *Put that cheese down! I've hardly begun. You ain't heard nothing yet!*

'The Celts were brilliant, Mum! They celebrated midwinter and midsummer and everything! And it's nearly midsummer now, isn't it?'

'That's right, love. Nice, long, light evenings.'

'The Celts, right, they had these parties. They were totally cool. They lit bonfires to chase away the evil spirits. And they sang and danced and stuff. Amazing! I did a painting of a Celt dancing and Mrs Jenkins said it was excellent and put it up on the wall.'

Mum looked up from her yogurts and a big smile broke out on her face. Praise for her baby! I'd softened her up nicely now.

'Oh, well done, love!'

I hurled myself at her, wrapping my arms tightly around her so she couldn't be distracted by onions or loo cleaner.

'Mum!' I fixed her with a desperate grin, trying to look saintly and wonderfully Celtic. 'Please can we have a sleepover? Oh per-lease! A Celtic one. We worked it all out at break. It was Yasmin's idea.'

Help! Mum's smile was gone. She looked down at me as though I was an annoying little dog and she was regretting rescuing me from the dog pound.

'Well, if it's Yasmin's idea, maybe Yasmin should invite you,' said Mum. 'I hate this sleepover business. We never had sleepovers when I was a girl. Just a nice little party and then home.'

'It's got to be us this time! Yasmin had a sleepover last month! And Hannah had one at Christmas! And Lauren had one when it snowed! And Froggo had one at Hallowe'en! It's my turn and unless I have one everyone will hate me!'

Mum sighed and prised my arms off her. She started to fiddle with the groceries again, but her whole mood had changed. All that Celtic stuff and the joys of midsummer and my brilliant success in the artistic world all counted for nothing

now. Now that I wanted to impose a gang of noisy kids on her, all night.

Dad entered the room. I flew at him and flung my arms round him instead. He looked puzzled. He could suss there were problems.

'Oh, please, Dad!' I yelled. 'I want to have a sleepover with a bonfire and dancing and singing!' I didn't mention the evil spirits. Mum doesn't believe in that sort of thing and gets cross when people talk about it. And Dad is scared of everything. 'I promise we'll go to bed and be quiet whenever you want us to!'

Dad looked at Mum and shrugged. Mum was actually frowning now. This was going badly.

'Who would be coming?' she demanded, putting her hands on her hips like a drawing of an angry washerwoman in a book of nursery rhymes.

'Nobody, much,' I said. 'Just Yasmin, and Hannah – and Lauren and Froggo – and Max and Toby and Grace and Emily and –'

'Stop, stop, Ruby!' snapped Mum. 'I'm not having boys, for a start!'

'But I went to Froggo's sleepover at Hallowe'en!' I begged. 'The girls slept in a separate room!'

'We haven't got a spare room!'

'The girls could sleep in my tree house and the boys could sleep on the floor!'

'You'd have a job squeezing two people into your tree house, let alone a whole gang!' Mum was putting the kettle on now, but in a nasty, sulky way. 'I've got enough to cope with at the moment! I've had to do extra shifts because of Alex being off with flu! I'm shattered!'

'Dad will organise it, then!' I yelled, hanging on to Dad in desperation and almost tearing his jumper.

'Don't drag me into it!' said Dad. 'Parties are women's work.'

'That's just typical of you, Brian!' cried Mum. Dad had only been joking really, but she was in a temper now and working up to a row. All I'd wanted was a tiny little sleepover, and now I was about to cause my parents a horrid divorce.

Mum stomped off upstairs to have a bath and Dad and I started to prepare the dinner. It was going to be potatoes in their jackets and salad. I scrubbed the spuds while Dad messed about with leaves. He grows a lot in his garden.

'Dad . . . ?' I asked. 'What do boys like? I mean, as a kind of treat – if Froggo and Max can't come to my sleepover, I've got to ask them to some other treat.'

A dreamy look came over Dad's face. I just knew he wasn't going to take this seriously.

'Making marmalade?' he suggested. 'Sewing little pairs of trousers for slightly cold dogs? Dressing up as elves and playing the flute in pink tights? That's the sort of thing I used to love when I was a boy.'

He laughed at his own joke, and I tried to cook up a smile. I had to humour him. We pricked the spuds and put them in the oven.

'No, seriously, Dad, what would boys like really?'

'A trip to the cinema to see a frightening movie? A martial arts number with a terrifying oriental girl who goes soaring up in the air like a whirling dervish and then cuts a monster's head off with

one flash of her sword? Excuse me, that's made me feel faint. I'll have to sit down.'

Dad was kidding, of course. Although he is kind of nervous and useless, he's not a total wuss. All this was just kidding along . . . *Kidding.* That was it! Maybe Froggo and Max and I could do something comedy-related.

'We could go and see a comedy film!' I yelled, jumping up and down.

Dad pulled a face. He was reading the small print on the margarine tub.

'We're going to have to stop getting this stuff,' he said. 'It's got hydrogenated fats in it.'

'Dad! Will you take me and Froggo and Max to a comedy film?' I asked. 'And buy us popcorn and stuff? I have to treat them to something because Mum won't let boys come to the sleepover.'

Dad looked at me with glazed eyes. He hadn't been listening. 'What?' he asked. 'When is this? What was that again?'

I knew I was going to have to sort this one out by myself.

'Nothing,' I said. 'Forget it.'

Dad looked guilty but relieved, and started to admire his radicchio leaves. They're a bit like red and white lettuce. They look beautiful but they taste terrible. Apparently children have a lot more taste buds than grown-ups, which is why we can be a bit more fussy about our food. Don't start me on spinach. Why would anybody want to eat something that tastes like a tree? I would rather eat a whole lampshade. Roasted, of course.

CHAPTER 3

You can all go and boil your heads!

ON THE WAY to school next morning my mind was racing. I had to tell Yasmin what Mum had said about the sleepover – that all those extra people couldn't come, just her and Lauren and Hannah. And we had to make sure the other people never found out. I hoped Yasmin hadn't told them about the sleepover already. She's such a gossipy gasbag.

Then I had to find out what Froggo would like as a treat. I'd have to do it secretly and like a spy.

What films he wanted to see, or whatever. Maybe he'd like some kind of boyish day out at a safari park or something. Max would tag along, whatever Froggo decided. I wondered if I ought to keep the sleepover a secret from Froggo and Max.

I wondered if I ought to keep the boyish event a secret from Yasmin, Hannah and Lauren. I thought perhaps I should. Yasmin can be very stressy about things like that. I could just imagine her demanding to come on the boyish treat as well. And I knew if she did, she would spoil it by wearing a pink skirt and talking about princesses.

The first person I met in the playground was Grace. She's a lovely girl with straight glossy black hair and big white teeth.

'Hi, Ruby!' she grinned, her teeth flashing in dazzling fashion. 'Want a piece of chocolate?'

I took a piece and said thank you. I was feeling terribly guilty. Grace wasn't going to be asked to my sleepover, even though she'd been on the original guest list. She didn't know, of course. Thank goodness! Poor Grace. She was so much nicer than me.

Although I suppose it could have been worse. I mean, I wasn't planning to kill her or anything. But that's kind of what it felt like, in a way.

Lauren came over. She can spot chocolate at three miles, and smell it in another country. I bet she raises her nose and sniffs the air sometimes and says, 'Yes . . . they're tucking into a gigantic Easter Egg in Russia, right now . . . on Spotsky Street, Moscow.'

I thought of what a weird word Moscow was. A cow covered in moss briefly flashed through my mind. Brains are such strange things. Mine was having visions of green cows at the very moment when it had to be concentrating on the vital business of stopping Lauren from mentioning my sleepover, if by chance Yasmin had mentioned it to her.

'Hi, Lauren, are you better today?' I asked. Lauren nodded.

'I had a tummy upset,' she said. 'But I'm fine now, in fact I'm starving.'

'Would you like a piece of chocolate?' asked Grace sweetly, even though it was her last piece and I just knew she'd been saving it up for break.

'Oh thanks! Delish!' Lauren grinned and gobbled it up right away. Grace looked a bit sad but heroic. I began to feel Grace was a much better person than Lauren or me. Though she can be very boring on the subject of a boy band called Flash Harry.

Suddenly I saw Yasmin running towards us. Disaster! She was bound to yell out, 'Ruby, did your mum say yes to the sleepover? Who are we gonna invite?' I had to act, and now.

I ran off, kind of beckoning Yasmin to follow. She chased me right into the corner where the cherry tree is.

'Ruby!' she puffed, laughing. 'What . . . ?'

'Shhhh!' I whispered. 'Listen! You're going to keep your big mouth shut, because this sleepover's going to have to be the biggest secret!'

'My mouth is so not big!' shouted Yasmin. The cherry tree practically shook.

'No, listen, Mum did say yes but I had to torment her for hours to agree to it. And we can't have boys, so you mustn't mention it to Froggo and Max. And we can't have Grace and Alice and Emily, so you mustn't mention it to them.'

'Well, who can we have, then?' said Yasmin, looking grumpy.

'It's going to be you and me and Hannah and Lauren,' I said. 'But Yasmin, it's got to be secret, OK? Got to be. Promise you won't tell anybody. Especially Froggo.'

'I promise,' said Yasmin. 'I'm not speaking to him anyway, since he threw custard in my hair.'

'OK,' I said. 'And we have to get Hannah and Lauren to promise not to mention it either.'

At this point Hannah and Lauren joined us and we all made a solemn vow never to mention the sleepover to anybody, even under torture.

'How are we going to be able to scare evil spirits away if there are only four of us?' growled Yasmin. 'It's hardly even a party at all, just the four of us.'

'Yes,' smiled Lauren. 'I mean, there are more than four of us just in my family!'

'OK, OK!' I snapped. 'No need to boast about your enormous families!' I was trying to make a joke of it, but I was a bit cross with Lauren for backing Yasmin up and dissing my sleepover. Usually she gives me support and is loyal.

'I think Ruby's sleepover sounds lovely,' said Hannah. 'Who wants horrid boys? I'm longing to sleep in Ruby's tree house. I can't wait.'

I smiled, but anxiously. Hannah was backing me up and being nice, but there just wasn't going to be room in the tree house for all four of us. I felt guilty about Hannah. She was so much nicer than me. Then she did it. She tossed her head and whipped her hair about – and it stung my eye.

'OK,' said Yasmin with a sigh, as if she was agreeing to go along with my sleepover, even though it was, by her standards, pathetic. 'What are we going to eat?'

It was none of her business what we were going to eat. But that's just like Yasmin. She always wants to organise everything. She's a power freak.

'Sausage and mash,' I said firmly. It's one of my favourite meals. Yasmin pulled a face.

'Sorry, Ruby,' she said. 'I can't eat pork. Sausages are made out of pork.'

'I can't eat sausages either,' said Hannah with disgust. 'I'm a vegetarian.'

'I can eat sausages, Ruby,' said Lauren anxiously. 'But I don't like mashed potato. Ordinary potato is all right. Chips, I mean, or baked spuds in their jackets. But I don't like plain boiled potatoes either, really. Sorry.'

Something in me snapped.

'You can all go and boil your heads!' I yelled, and ran off across the yard in a blinding fury. Already this sleepover was giving me such grief, I couldn't bear it. Already I hated the three guests, even though only a few hours ago they'd been my favourite people. If only I was a monkey in the rainforest! I bet they don't have this kind of trouble with their sleepovers.

But my troubles were only just beginning, because up ahead I could see Froggo and Max doing some boyish fighting stuff with their schoolbags. I had to think of some kind of treat for them and keep it secret from the girls. Gosh! I was exhausted, and the bell hadn't even gone for registration.

CHAPTER 4
Help, help, help!

I RAN UP TO Froggo and Max. 'Stop that stupid fighting!' I yelled. 'Why do boys like fighting? It's the only thing they ever do! Violence! That's all they understand! Name me one thing – one thing – that boys would enjoy that doesn't involve ripping something or some-body to pieces!'

It was a bit blatant, but with any luck they wouldn't notice. Froggo and Max stopped hitting each other and stood there, panting and thinking.

'Come on, guys!' I taunted them. 'When have

you ever had fun without hitting something or somebody?'

'I peed over a garden wall once,' said Max. 'It was great! There was an old lady in there and she looked up and said, "That's odd! They didn't forecast rain!"' The boys cracked up about this for an eternity.

'Listen,' I said. 'Imagine I'm your fairy godmother! I can wave my magic wand and give you three wishes. What would they be?'

'A visit to the NASA space centre!' said Max. 'Experience Blast Off!' And he somehow turned into a rocket with his arms pressed tight against his sides. He was rumbling and sizzling and you could almost see steam escaping from his shoes.

'You sad nerd!' yelled Froggo. 'Who wants to go to Houston when you can go to the moon? No – let's go to that new planet they've just discovered that's a bit like Earth! That would be well cool! Come on, take us there – it's only 120 trillion miles!'

'Zero gravity!' yelled Max. 'Amazing! If you did a poo, the poo would just float about round your head!'

I began to feel that providing boys with a treat was going to be quite a challenge.

'OK,' I sighed. 'Your first wish is space travel complete with flying poo. What's the second?'

'Kidnap J. K. Rowling!' shouted Froggo. 'And force her to go on writing Harry Potter books for ever and ever and ever!'

At last, a realistic suggestion.

'You sad nerd, Frogger!' said Max with a sneer. 'Don't just read the books! Live the dream!' He sounded like a TV advert for something. 'Go to Hogwarts!! Jump on that broomstick! Fly across the sky in five seconds flat!' And Max jumped aboard an imaginary broomstick and charged off across the yard.

'OK,' I said. I felt like giving up, but I had to hang on in there. Maybe Froggo's third wish would be something I really could provide. Although in the back of my mind I was already busy with Plan B – working out how to kidnap J. K. Rowling. 'Come on, Frogs – what's your third wish? And don't be so mad this time.'

Froggo was looking across the yard to where Max was still zooming about.

'Promise you won't tell Max,' he said kind of furtively, like a spy.

I was startled. What was this about?

'I promise,' I said. Max couldn't hear us anyway

– he was about fifty trillion miles away already.

'My mum says do you want to come to a barbecue on Saturday?' said Froggo quickly, still watching Max. 'She says Max can't come because last time he came to our house he did something rude. My cousin Natasha's coming – you remember her?'

'Yeah, Natasha's cool!' I said. But inside I was panicking. Here was lovely old Froggo, inviting me to a family barbecue on the very night I was planning to have a sleepover! How could I explain that I couldn't go to his barbecue without revealing that I was having a sleepover? And he wasn't invited to my sleepover, even though he'd invited me to his sleepover last Hallowe'en – *and* his barbecue.

'You can eat your own weight in sausages!' Froggo grinned. 'And we're going to have a treasure hunt!'

Froggo's barbecue already sounded amazing, heaps better than my boring old sleepover. I didn't know what to say so I just sort of jumped up and down, screaming into my hands and yelling, 'Brilliant, brilliant, brilliant!'

'I'll take that as a yes, then,' said Froggo, and then he suddenly took off across the playground in the manner of a 4x4 vehicle driving up a rocky mountain road.

I stopped jumping up and down and started biting my hands in secret agony. What had I done? Froggo thought I had accepted his invite, but on the very same night I was supposed to be having Yasmin, Lauren and Hannah round!

Why hadn't I done something really sensible and told Froggo I was going to be visiting my grandma? Now it was too late. I was double-booked. This was a catastrophe.

Who could get me out of this jam? I could only think of one person: my bodyguard, my guardian angel, my fairy godmother (part-time anyway), the amazing Holly Helvellyn. I whipped out my mobile and started texting. I couldn't sort this problem out myself. I needed help.

DR HOL, my text went, *GT MSELF INTO V V STPD JAM. DSPRTELY NEED UR ADVICE. HELP, HELP, HELP! LV RUBY*

I sent the text off, crossed my fingers and prayed for Holly to come up with some brilliant idea. Moments later her reply came back.

U THNK UV GT PROBS? MY LIFE IN RUINS. WILL MEET U AFTA SCH TDAY. MAYBE WE CN RUN AWA TOGETHA. LOVE HOL.

Ohmigawd! Holly had problems too! I hoped that horrid ex-boyfriend of hers, Dom, wasn't giving her grief. If he was, I'd bite his ankles. I'd pay Max to pee all over him from a great height.

I'd been hoping for ages that one day Holly would get together with my foul bro Joe, but I don't see any signs of it. Whenever they meet there's what you call 'an atmosphere'. I think it's because of Joe's girlfriend Tiffany. I never know whether Tiffany and Joe are an item or not. They're always rowing and dumping each other. I'm sure he'd be much happier with Holly. But what can you do?

At least I was going to see Holly after school.

That would be brilliant. If only we could run away together! I wouldn't mind being her slave if we could live on a desert island.

Suddenly the bell rang and my dreams of a tropical life with Holly were shattered. I had to face the here and now. And suddenly I remembered that I had even more problems than I thought. We were about to have a maths test. The perfect start to the school day.

CHAPTER 5

But what am I going to do?

A FEW HOURS LATER, Holly was waiting for me outside the school gates.

'OK, text your mum and tell her I'm taking you out to tea at the Dolphin Cafe,' she said.

Brilliant! Today was turning into a treat after all, even though the maths test had been grim and I'd spent the day trying to stop Yasmin from shouting about my sleepover, and not to mention Froggo's barbecue to Max – or anyone else.

On the way to the cafe I told Holly all about it. She listened sympathetically.

'Listen, Ruby, this isn't a problem,' she said. 'Tell Froggo you're sorry, you got the dates wrong. You thought he meant the week after, or something. Or change the date of your sleepover.'

'I can't,' I explained. 'It has to be Midsummer's Day because Yasmin wants to do weird Celtic spells and stuff.'

'That girl is a such a legend!' sighed Holly. I felt jealous for a minute, even though Holly has said I'm a legend too, in the past. 'I wish I was coming to your sleepover, Ruby!'

'Why don't you come?' I yelled, suddenly seeing how my boring old party could be transformed by having Holly there being amazing all over the place.

'No, no!' said Holly, waving her arms about frantically. 'I can't! I wish I was ten years old but those days have gone! I really envy you, though – having a fabulous girls-only sleepover. You could have makeovers, too. Then it could be a sleepmakeover. Or a sleepover makeover. And you could have apple turnovers and popovers.'

I've never been even a tiny little bit interested in makeovers, so for once I didn't go for Holly's suggestion.

'It's a nightmare,' I said. 'I don't know what food

to have. Hannah's a vegetarian and Yasmin's a Muslim and Lauren hardly eats anything except chocolate. And I hate spinach.'

'I don't think spinach is compulsory at sleepovers, Ruby!' said Holly, laughing. 'Actually I don't like it as a food, either, but I adore it as a colour.'

'But what am I going to do?' I wailed. 'Nobody likes the same food as anybody else!'

'Get them to bring their own picnic, then,' said Holly crisply as we reached the Dolphin Cafe. 'If they must be obsessed with food fads, let them bring their own horrid little sarnies of boiled eggs with grass and locusts or whatever.'

I laughed. My problems did seem to be disappearing. Holly was so brilliant. Just wait till I told Mum about the bring-your-own-picnic idea! And we could all eat our picnics out on the lawn, while the moon came up. Then we could do the spells and stuff.

We entered the cafe. Now for a treat! I could smell the freshly baked cheese scones.

'Holly!' A shout went up from a table by the window. It was Jess Jordan and a boy with short hair and a long, kind of joky face. 'And Ruby!' Jess waved us over and moved her bag off a chair. 'Sit with us!' she commanded. 'Fred, this is Ruby Rogers. Ruby, this is Fred Parsons.'

Fred did a huge exaggerated smile at me, as if I was about two years old. I ignored him. Holly asked what I wanted.

'A ginger beer and a cheese scone, please,' I said politely. It was such a shame Jess and Fred were here. I wanted Holly all to myself.

'Ruby Rogers! You could be a cowboy with a name like that,' said Fred. 'Is your horse tied up outside?'

'Ha ha! Shut up, Parsons!' said Jess, elbowing him in the ribs. 'I babysat for Ruby once, and guess what?! There was a power cut, and I hid in the cupboard under the stairs, and Ruby came downstairs and I heard her pad-padding about, and I thought she was a serial killer, and I was scared out of my seven wits!'

'Are you a serial killer?' asked Fred, staring at me seriously. His eyes were huge and grey. I knew he was making fun of me but it was in a weird kind of way. I didn't think I liked him.

'I might be a gangster when I leave school,' I said.

'Oh, gang warfare's much more fun than serial killing,' said Fred, turning to Jess and putting on a

clever professor-type voice. 'Whereas the serial killer is a loner, outside society, the gang member may evolve from crime into jam-making or the knitting of cardigans.'

Jess giggled and hit Fred again. She seemed to hit him a lot, but with love, somehow. 'Ruby is Joe Rogers' little sister,' she said. Fred looked impressed.

'He's a legend,' said Fred. 'Joe Rogers. He stood on my foot once in a crowd. I was so grateful! I didn't clean my shoes for a year. Yesss! Joe Rogers . . . Ashcroft School's answer to Damian Hirst.'

'Who's Damian Hirst?' I asked.

'A famous artist,' said Jess. 'I don't think that's very flattering, though. I think Joe is Ashcroft

School's answer to Michelangelo. Have you heard of Michelangelo, Ruby?'

'Yes,' I said, though it was a slight lie. I had nearly heard of him, anyway. I hate the way, when you're with older people, especially some teenagers, you become kind of trapped and very stupid. Luckily I don't feel like this with Holly, and soon she was back with my ginger beer and her hot chocolate.

'This is my last meal,' she said, waving a massive baguette packed with cheese and salad. 'Cos tomorrow morning I've got to have two teeth out! My God! I'm terrified!'

'Oh, bad luck,' said Jess.

'I've got too many teeth!' Holly frowned as she chewed. 'I'm, like, so terrified I'm planning to run away!' She didn't mention the fact that she'd said she'd like to run away with *me*. I suppose that would be uncool or something.

Anyway, now I knew what Holly's problem was. I'd thought it was her ex, Dom, giving her grief, but it turned out to be just the dentist. I couldn't give her any advice or sympathy, though, because Jess and Fred were talking so much I couldn't get a word in. I just went on sadly eating my cheese scone and wishing it was just me and Holly.

'My grandad had seven teeth out once,' Jess was saying. 'And Granny says they had to hold him down in the chair!'

'Thanks for that encouraging little anecdote, Jess!' growled Holly.

'Did you know,' said Fred, 'that the roots of the wisdom teeth go right down into your feet? I mean, the nerves do. Maybe you should try acupuncture. In China, they could remove your appendix without you feeling a thing. You could be sitting up sipping tea and watching TV. They just put a little needle in the back of your hand, and it acts as a nerve block.'

'Needles! Don't mention needles!' screamed Holly, covering her ears.

After that they started talking about various bands, and I stopped listening. Instead, I started worrying about my sleepover again and the fact that, on that very same night, I'd agreed to go to Froggo's barbecue. I know Holly had said I just had to fess up to Froggo and tell him I'd got mixed up about the dates, but it wasn't quite as simple as that.

What made it worse was that they weren't inviting masses of guests to the barbecue, it was kind of just me, so I was almost like a guest of honour or something. I had to be there for Natasha!

'Ten pence for your thoughts, Ruby,' said Jess, suddenly noticing I was frowning.

I explained the situation.

'No problem, young lady!' Fred whooped. 'I'll go to the barbecue, disguised as you. Problem solved.'

'You are a total idiot, Parsons!' scolded Jess, pinching his arm. I looked at Holly, hoping she would think it was time to go, but she was looking thoughtful and fiddling with her teeth.

It was clear that this time she wasn't going to be my fairy godmother. I was on my own.

CHAPTER 6
You're just a control freak!

ONCE I'D FINISHED my homework that night, I started to rack my brains – although they were still slightly racked from the homework. We'd had to write an imaginary diary in the character of a Celtic child. You know the kind of thing . . .

Woke up in hut. Hard-boiled seagull's egg for breakfast. Yuk. Dad went off to fight the tribe next door – known as the Picts. Had to help Mum sweep the hut. V. dusty. Had asthma attack. Alas, inhalers not yet invented. Hard-boiled seagull's egg for lunch. Dad came home with blood on his cloak. Our tribe won! Yesss! Us 3, Picts 0 after extra time.

I couldn't write it like that really. It had to be serious. The Celts were ever so serious. They had four hundred gods. One of them was called Rhiannon, which is my mum's name. Rhiannon was goddess of the moon. I started to draw a moon on the back of my notebook. The moon had a sulky face. In fact, it looked a bit like me.

I had to stop feeling bad about things and work out a way of solving the problem. I got out a piece of clean paper. I wrote down:

Froggo's barbecue.

My sleepover.

For a while I just stared at those two sentences. This was hardly what you'd call progress. Then I jotted down a few ideas.

Make an excuse at the last minute so I don't have to go to Froggo's barbecue. Tell him I've got a headache.

The trouble is, I knew that Froggo's mum would ring my mum to discuss the details of my visit, so I wouldn't be able to get away with a lie. The mums would be sure to talk to each other. I didn't want to spend the rest of my life keeping my mum away from Froggo's mum. Especially as I plan to marry him if there's nobody else available — if I marry anybody, which is unlikely.

Ask Froggo to change the date of his barbecue.

This was also rubbish. Guests just don't do that sort of thing, do they?

Tell Froggo my mum says I can't go to his barbecue.

But why? Why? Why?

Because I have something else I've got to do. Like host a sleepover — to which you're not invited, incidentally!

Nice one. Froggo probably wouldn't speak to me again, ever. Even when we're married.

I sighed such a deep, sad, horrible sigh that I pulled a muscle in my chest. This was awful! How could I get out of it? My head was beginning to ache, what with all the racking of brains, and I was feeling a bit sick. I knew this much: I'd rather be sick all night in glorious technicolour than tell Froggo I couldn't go to his barbecue, especially after jumping up and down and saying, 'Brilliant, brilliant, brilliant!'

Suddenly I heard a sound. Raised voices. It sounded like Joe and Tiffany having a tiff — I think that's why she's called Tiff, by the way.

Mum and Dad had gone out to see a neighbour, and when they're out, Joe and Tiffany are, well, louder, sometimes.

'You should have told me!' That was Joe's voice booming. When he's cross his voice sounds like a foghorn.

'I forgot, OK? I've got a lot on my mind! Revision, yeah? For exams! Some people aren't geniuses like you! Some people have to, like, work!'

'All you had to do was tell me! You can't just say I'm going somewhere without even asking me!'

'So what else are you going to be doing? What? What?'

'Anything! Anything! I just want to be in charge of my own life!'

'You're just a control freak, Joe Rogers!'

'That's crap! Absolute crap! All I'm saying is, I want to be in control of my own life! I want you to stop arranging things behind my back and tell me what's going on!'

I wanted them to stop shouting, so I stomped loudly out of my room and went into the bath-room. I slammed the door so they would hear I was around. A moment later, some deafening rap music broke out. Joe often puts it on when he's having a row with Tiffany, to cover the sound of them shouting. It's a bit like a modern, very horrible sort of musical or opera.

I couldn't get Joe's words out of my head. *All you had to do was tell me!* I had to tell Froggo. Boys didn't like being left in the dark, that was obvious. Well, nobody does, do they?

I had to tell Froggo the truth. The whole truth. Even the bit about him not being able to be invited to my sleepover because he was a boy. My heart was hammering away like mad as I walked downstairs and approached the phone.

Please, please, help me, Guardian Angel, I prayed. Sometimes, when things get really serious, like when Mum had to go into hospital, I think Joe's my guardian angel. But the rest of the time he acts more like my personal torturer. And anyway, your guardian angel can't keep his eye on the ball when he's having a row with his girlfriend, can he?

I picked up the phone and dialled Froggo's number. My hands were shaking like mad and my mouth had gone strangely dry. I heard the phone ringing. I prayed for everybody to be out. I had my speech ready. *I'm so sorry, Froggo, but I won't be able to come to your barbecue after all. I'd forgotten* (that bit was the only lie) *that I'm having a sleepover that night. I'm so, so sorry.*

'Hi!' a cheery man's voice answered. It was Froggo's dad.

'Hello, this is Ruby Rogers,' I said politely, exactly as trained by Mum. 'Could I speak to Fr— Dan, please?'

'Sure . . . Dan! It's your girlfriend!'

I cringed massively. How dare Dan's dad say that? The phone went quiet, then Froggo picked up.

'Sorry about that,' he said. 'My dad's got a weird sense of humour.' He sounded really embarrassed.

'Frogs, the barbecue . . .' I croaked. My voice had almost given way.

'Oh yeah, the barbecue.' Froggo sounded even more embarrassed. He was kind of in a hurry to say something. 'I'm sorry, I forgot to tell you something about that. The barbecue's at lunchtime, OK? But that evening we're all going to go out for a family-type dinner sort of thing, because it's my grandpa's birthday. So Mum says would it be all right if we take you home about four o'clock?'

Froggo sounded stiff with embarrassment, but my head nearly flew round the room by itself with sheer delight.

'That would be perfect!' I said. 'Perfect! It fits in

totally brilliantly with other stuff I have to do later! Thanks so much!'

'It's OK, then?' said Froggo warily.

'Yes! Yes! Mega!'

'Good,' said Froggo, sounding immensely relieved. Hah! If he thought he was relieved, he should see me!

We said goodbye, and then I literally danced round the kitchen, singing, 'Hoorah, hoorah, hoorah! Yess, yess, yess! Result!'

Thank you, Guardian Angel – you are the best ever! I thought. How could things have turned out more brilliantly? Froggo's event would be over by the afternoon, and he couldn't have come to my sleepover anyway, because of his grandpa's birthday party! Now I could relax and enjoy myself and concentrate on making my sleepover the best ever.

Just then the phone rang again. It made me jump. I picked it up warily, hoping it wasn't Froggo's dad offering to hold our wedding reception at Alton Towers.

'Ruby!' It was Yasmin. 'Listen! I've had a huge row with Hannah! I'm never speaking to her again as long as I live! So if you still want her to come to your sleepover, I'm sorry, but count me out!'

My world tumbled about my ears. I'd thought my problems were all sorted out, but it seemed they were only just beginning.

CHAPTER 7

What's the matter?

'WHAT'S THE ROW about?' I asked. I'd always thought Yasmin and Hannah got on really well. If Yasmin was going to get stressy with anybody, I'd expect it to be me – or Lauren. Yasmin's always a bit jealous about her.

'I went back to Hannah's for tea, right?' yelled Yasmin. I had to hold the phone away from my ear. 'And she showed me all this Celtic magic stuff she's got in her room. She was saying she's going to do spells to make Max marry her and other weird stuff. And that is so my idea! Hannah would never have got interested in this Celtic stuff if it hadn't been for me.'

In a way, Yasmin was being a big baby. I mean, if we learn about something at school, it's for everybody, isn't it? I did sympathise, though. I know what it feels like when somebody is copying you.

'It's like when I was holiday,' I said, 'and Sasha bought that monkey, just because I was interested in monkeys. She was a pain.'

'Yes, but you never have to see Sasha again!' snapped Yasmin. 'I have to see Hannah every day! You've got to tell her she can't come to your sleepover!'

'I can't do that!' I wailed. 'This is your problem, Yas, not mine. Give it a day or two. I'm sure you two will be friends again. See what happens tomorrow. I bet you she'll come up and say sorry.'

'Well, if she does, I'm gonna spit in her eye!' shouted Yasmin. She loves big rows. I cringed.

'Don't lose it,' I warned her. 'OK, so she probably only got interested in that Celtic stuff because you did. But that's just because she, like, admires you or whatever.' Mum had explained to me on holiday that the only reason Sasha bought that monkey was because she thought I was cool with my monkeys and stuff.

'You're on her side!' yelled Yasmin. 'You like Hannah more than me!'

'Don't be an idiot!' I flared up. 'Of course I don't like her more than you! In fact, I sometimes think you like her more than me!'

'That's crap! And anyway, you like Lauren better than me too!'

'Yasmin, don't be stupid. You know I –'

'Don't tell me I'm stupid! You just said I was an idiot! You're the one who's an idiot! And I don't want to come to your stupid sleepover anyway!'

Yasmin slammed the phone down. I was stunned. This had blown up out of nothing. When I had first answered the phone, she'd just been mad at Hannah. Now she was in the most terrific strop with me. I sighed deeply. It felt as though my heart had sunk right down to the floor. I dragged myself over to the sofa, collapsed on to it and flicked the remote.

It was one of those wildlife programmes. There was a beautiful bird displaying his tail and making the most amazing sounds. David Attenborough was saying '. . . *we found a lyrebird singing of its own doom.*' The bird was imitating the sounds of foresters with chainsaws working nearby as they felled its forest – destroying its home.

Two big tears rolled down my cheeks. Why do we waste time arguing about stupid unimportant things when such a beautiful, brilliant bird was in danger?

I heard Joe's bedroom door burst open and feet thundering down the stairs.

'You are such a plonker!' yelled Tiffany. 'I'll go on my own! It'll be way more fun without you anyway!' She rushed out and slammed the front door.

Joe didn't reply. I heard his door close with a fierce, hurt snap, and shortly afterwards really loud aggressive music came pumping out.

It seemed as if the whole world was just full of

aggro and hate. And the poor lyre bird just went on singing on TV, waving his beautiful plumes about. Birds and animals are just a hundred per cent better than we are. Humans suck. I hope we all go extinct soon. Especially Tiffany.

I decided to watch *The Simpsons* until Mum and Dad came home. I'd made a big decision. I knew what I had to do. It was the only way out of this jam. I was going to have to tell Mum and Dad to cancel my sleepover.

After a while I heard Mum's key in the lock. I got up off the sofa and went out into the hall. I wasn't sure what to say. Mum was bound to be cross because I'd pestered her about the sleepover so much in the first place. Now, asking for it to be cancelled was going to make her really mad.

'Oh, hello, love,' she said, as if she'd forgotten about me for a while. 'Did you finish your homework?'

'Yes, yes,' I said.

Dad closed the front door and took off his jacket. He didn't smile or joke or anything. Something was wrong. I forgot about my sleepover for a minute.

'What's the matter?' I asked. 'Don't tell me you've had a row too.'

'No, no,' said Mum. 'What do you mean, *too*?'

'Oh, Tiffany was here earlier,' I said. 'She and Joe had a blazing row and she called him rude names and went off. And slammed the door.'

'That's the spirit,' said Dad as a kind of joke, but not a very good one. 'Tea?' he asked Mum. She nodded wearily.

'What's the matter?' I insisted. Mum heaved a deep sigh and went through into the kitchen. She sat down at the table and kind of brushed absent-mindedly at some crumbs, as if she was thinking of something else.

'I got a call on my mobile while we were out,' she said. 'It's Auntie Megan. She's had a stroke.'

I felt a stab of terrible fear.

'Is she going to die?' I asked.

'They think not,' said Mum. 'I talked to her neighbour, you know, Gwen. She's in hospital. Gwen says the next couple of days will be critical.'

I wished Mum had lied and told me Auntie Megan was certain to live. Instead she'd talked to me as if I was a grown-up. Sometimes I like that, but not this time.

'I'll have to take tomorrow off,' said Mum. 'Dad and I will drive up to see her. It's such a long journey . . .' Auntie Megan lives in North Wales. 'I think you should stay here with Joe. What do you think?'

If I'd had to go off to North Wales with Mum and Dad, that would have been the perfect excuse to cancel my sleepover. But I felt guilty even thinking like that – even for a split second. It was as if Auntie Megan's horrible stroke was just kind of a useful excuse for me instead of a horrendous crisis for all of us. But sometimes you can't help the horrible things that cross your mind.

For a moment I wanted to go with Mum and Dad. Then I had second thoughts.

'I don't want to come,' I said. 'I hate hospitals and I don't want to see Auntie ill or – anything.'

'No, no, love,' said Mum. 'You stay here with Joe. I'll go up and have a word with him.'

Mum went upstairs. Dad made the tea. I didn't know whether to mention my sleepover or not.

'Dad . . .' I said. 'This means I have to cancel my sleepover, doesn't it?'

Dad looked vague and absent-minded.

'Oh no, Rube,' he said. 'Joe can keep you all in order. Don't start pestering Mum about that now. She's feeling a bit fragile.'

So I didn't mention it. I just had some hot chocolate and went to bed. I prayed that Auntie Megan would be all right. I prayed that the lyre bird of southern Australia would be all right. I didn't mention my sleepover. I figured that God had got enough on his plate.

CHAPTER 8
How awful!

I COULDN'T SLEEP that night. Auntie Megan is such a big part of my life. I always long for the summer hols when we go and spend a week with her. She lives in a fantastic part of North Wales, with mountains and woods and the sea. And she is so utterly lovely. She's Mum's aunt really, so she's a bit like an extra granny, but she's very young for a granny because she was the youngest in her family.

I had that sick feeling of dread that I'd felt when Mum went into hospital and I didn't know if she'd come out again. In the end I managed to get some sleep, but I had horrid dreams about trying to wade across a swamp. In another dream Hannah and Yasmin were fighting, and then, when I tried to separate them they kind of fell to bits and turned into pools of liquid and ran away into cracks in the ground.

When I went down to breakfast I felt tired. Mum looked pale and Dad was taking some aspirin. Joe was staring kind of gloomily at his muesli. He'd probably had nightmares, too, about Tiffany strangling him or something.

'I've rung Gwen this morning,' said Mum, 'and apparently Megan got through the night all right, but we're planning to leave right away because you never know with strokes. You look pale, Ruby – are you all right, love?'

'Yes,' I said. 'Fine.'

'Right. Now listen, Joe.' Joe looked up in a sulky way. 'I'm leaving you in charge, right? It's your job to look after Ruby. We'll be back on Sunday.'

'OK,' said Joe. He didn't sound very thrilled about it, but I knew he'd be feeling awful about Auntie Megan too. He went to stay with her while I was being born. And she's always said he is her favourite boy in all the world, and baked his favourite chocolate cake every time we go there.

'Right, Brian, have you packed a few things?' Mum went off upstairs to see to the cases. Dad slurped the last of his tea and then followed her. They were totally focused on their journey. I could see that it would be stupid even to mention my sleepover.

'I was supposed to be having a sleepover tomorrow night,' I said to Joe.

He pulled a kind of mock horrified face.

'You can forget that for a start,' he growled.

It was, in a way, the perfect excuse. Mum and Dad having to go off to see Auntie Megan was a crisis. Everybody would understand if I cancelled. Huge relief flooded through me. I was going to tell Yasmin and Hannah and Lauren to forget it – until another time. It would be the easiest thing in the world.

'Oh good,' I said. 'I never really wanted one anyway.' Joe wasn't listening. I wondered if he was thinking about Tiffany or Auntie Megan. I had a horrible feeling he was going to be in a fit of the glooms all weekend.

When I got to school I looked around for Yasmin. OK, we'd had a row last night, but we'd had worse rows. We'd had rows that went on for days and days. We'd had rows that were so poisonous, it was as if a black cloud was hanging over the whole town. What we'd had last night was just a little shouting match. It would be easy enough to make friends again.

Lauren ran up. Well, she skipped up, actually. I'd hardly ever seen her look so happy.

'Guess what, Ruby!' she said. 'Last night Mum and I baked some cakes for your sleepover party! Mum said she knew how busy your mum is, so it was the least she could do. We made chocolate brownies and those little iced buns that you love! And we made some gingerbread Celts! And guess what! We decorated those with actual Celtic symbols on the icing! We found them in a book Mum's got about history!'

My mouth went dry. I smiled, somehow, because it would have been very rude not to. Lauren put her arm round me and kind of strolled round the playground. My legs felt weak, like a rag doll's, but I managed to totter along beside her. Lauren was so excited that she didn't notice I was a bit quiet.

'Oh, Ruby, I so can't wait to spend the whole night in your tree house!' she babbled. 'It will be so, so, so wonderful! I couldn't sleep last night I

was so excited! I've been counting the hours. I know it's silly, but I haven't looked forward to anything so much, ever. It'll be brilliant! Did your dad say we could have a bonfire?'

'It's a little bit – uh, tr-tricky,' I stammered. 'I'm not sure about the bonfire, because – well, my mum and dad have had to go to Wales to see my auntie. She's in hospital.'

'Oh no!' Lauren's face fell. 'How awful! Does that mean we have to cancel the sleepover?'

I saw huge tears well up in her eyes. Her lip kind of trembled. How could I break her heart, especially after all that Celtic baking?

'No, no, the sleepover's still on,' I said quickly. 'Joe will be looking after us. Not that we need looking after. In fact, we'll be looking after him, I should think. Tiffany walked out on him again last night.'

'Oh, I don't think I'll ever have a boyfriend!' said Lauren, shuddering. 'All those rows!'

'It's not Joe and Tiffany's row we need to worry about,' I said. 'It's Hannah's and Yasmin's. Yas rang me last night and said I had to tell Hannah she couldn't come to my sleepover because they'd had this massive row, and when I tried to reason with her she hung up on me.'

Lauren's eyes looked huge.

'Oh no!' she whispered. 'If anything happens to spoil the sleepover, I think I'll die! It's going to be the best thing ever!'

'Don't worry,' I said, squeezing her hand. 'Nothing's going to spoil it, I promise.' I've always felt as if it's my job to look after Lauren a bit, ever since she arrived at school as a new girl, looking all awkward and shy. But now the wretched sleepover was back on the agenda, I was starting to feel sick with worry again. Somehow I had to make things up with Yasmin, and then get Hannah and Yasmin back together, and then persuade Joe to let us have the sleepover, and make sure everybody had a brilliant time. Just thinking about it made me feel exhausted.

CHAPTER 9
Go away! I hate you!

WHEN WE LINED up to go in for registration, Yasmin totally blanked me. And when we got to our classroom, she went over to the other side of the room and sat next to Grace. Hannah came over and sat with me and Lauren, which only made it look as if we were ganging up on Yasmin.

'Yasmin won't speak to me, Ruby!' Hannah whispered in anguish, while Mrs Jenkins was busy fiddling with her books and papers.

'Join the club!' I whispered back. I tried to catch

Yasmin's eye and smile, to break the ice, but she never once looked in our direction.

'Oh dear!' whispered Lauren. 'Yasmin looks really stressy! We must make friends with her again by the end of today or the sleepover will be ruined!'

At last the bell rang for break. Yasmin was one of the first to leave – she marched out quickly with Grace.

'Let's follow her!' said Lauren. 'I can offer her a bit of my chocolate!'

'I'll tell her I'm sorry,' fussed Hannah. 'I'll tell her I'm really, really sorry and beg her to be friends again.' She tossed her hair about frantically. I ducked.

'Listen!' I snapped. Suddenly I felt angry. 'I'm sick of Yasmin's moods! If she doesn't come over and apologise to us, I don't care. We'll have the sleepover without her.'

Lauren and Hannah looked a bit scared.

We went outside and shared Lauren's chocolate. Across the yard, I could see Yasmin sharing her divine cheese sandwiches with Grace.

Just think, if I had grabbed Yasmin that morning the moment she appeared and forced her to be friends again, one of those sandwiches could have been mine. OK, Lauren's chocolate was nice, but I'm not a chocoholic like she is. I've got a savoury tooth, not a sweet tooth. It's all part of being a tomboy, I suppose. I even ate an olive once without shrieking.

Yasmin ignored us all through break, and all through the next lessons, and all through the lunch hour. We tried to look as if we were enjoying ourselves. Hannah spent most of the lunch break braiding Lauren's hair into dreadlocks. Froggo zoomed past.

'Great hair, dude!' he yelled in his Bart Simpson voice. 'You look like Lennox Lewis!'

'Who's Lennox Lewis?' asked Lauren.

'He's the greatest heavyweight boxer there ever was!' shouted Froggo. 'He's a legend!'

Lauren looked a bit upset about this, but it was too late to do anything about the braids, because the bell went for afternoon school. Froggo zoomed up close to my ear.

'Don't forget the barbecue tomorrow!' he hissed. 'It starts at twelve at my place! Well, obviously! We wouldn't have a barbecue anywhere else, would we? Max still doesn't know, so keep your mouth shut!'

I nodded and tried to look delighted, even though I had actually totally forgotten about Froggo's barbecue. Horrors! Thank goodness he'd reminded me. What if I'd just forgotten to go and they'd rung and said, 'Where are you, Ruby? We've been waiting for you for an hour and a half!'?

Through afternoon school I was feeling increasingly desperate. Yasmin still hadn't even looked in my direction. It had been a mistake to leave her to make the first move. I'd forgotten how brilliant she is at sulking. What if she went off home without saying a word to me? It was Friday today. The sleepover was supposed to be tomorrow.

If I hadn't been having a sleepover, I could have toughed it out with Yasmin. I could have waited to see how long she would keep up the sulking. But the sleepover would be rubbish without her. She's always the life and soul of the party. She'd just got this great kind of festive personality. She really knows how to have fun.

I decided I had to grab Yasmin at home time. I watched the clock. A couple of minutes before the bell rang, I made sure everything was ready in my bag. I was totally focused. I was sure Yasmin would make a dash for it.

The bell rang. Mrs Jenkins dismissed us. Yasmin jumped to her feet.

I ran after her. She had been sitting right next to the door, so she had a head start. I had to push past everybody. Froggo got in the way. I got tangled up with Max and Charlie.

By the time I got out of the classroom, Yasmin had disappeared. I headed straight for the main door.

I saw Yasmin's back racing out across the schoolyard towards the gate. I had to stop her.

'Yasmin!' I yelled. 'Yasmin!'

She didn't turn round. Instead she ran faster.

'Yas!' I screamed. 'Wait a minute!'

Then somehow Yasmin tripped over her own bag and fell head first on to the ground. I hurried over to her.

'Yas! Yas!' I said. She raised her head and looked at her hands. Her palms were grazed and bleeding. Her chin was bleeding too. She started to cry.

'Are you all right? Are you all right?' I asked. I put my arm round her. She shrugged me off angrily.

'Go away!' she wailed. 'I hate you!'

Other people were coming up now. Yasmin's mum arrived and helped Yasmin to her feet, making cooing motherly sounds.

'Wanna go home!' sobbed Yasmin. 'Wanna go home!'

'Yes, yes, baby, we're going,' said Mrs Saffet. 'Come on, don't cry, be a brave girl. Would you like to come with us, Ruby?'

I didn't know what to say. It would be madness to go home for tea with Yasmin after she'd spent all day ignoring me and clearly blamed me for her accident. But I couldn't just leave her like this.

CHAPTER 10

You *are* stupid!

'YASMIN AND I had a row,' I said, panicking. I couldn't just pretend nothing had happened.

'Goodness me, we can't have that!' Mrs Saffet beamed. She is so lovely. 'Come home with us and have a liddle bit of tea, and we'll soon patch things up again, won't we?' I hesitated. Would Yasmin only hate me more for this? 'Won't we, baby?' cooed Mrs Saffet, cuddling Yasmin to her side and stroking her hair. Yasmin snuggled in close to her mum's side and nodded. She was still crying.

First we went back into school, to the girls' cloakrooms, and washed Yasmin's hands and chin. Mrs Jenkins appeared – somebody must have told her – and she offered Mrs Saffet some plasters for Yasmin's poor hands.

'Now, Ruby,' said Mrs Saffet, once we were climbing into her car, 'we must phone your parents and let them know you're coming to our house for tea.'

'My parents are in Wales, it's OK,' I said. I told her all about Auntie Megan's stroke as we drove home. Yasmin stared gloomily out of the window and looked as if she wasn't listening. It was going to be hard work making up with her, especially now she was hurt.

Back at Yasmin's house, there was a fantastic smell. Yasmin's mum had been baking.

'I finished my work early,' she said with a smile. Mrs Saffet has got a *very* sweet tooth. 'I made a lemon drizzle cake. How about that, eh, Yasmin?'

'Nice,' said Yasmin. But her voice sounded very small and kind of cracked.

'Now,' said Mrs Saffet, 'I want you two to go upstairs. Yasmin, change out of your school clothes. And when you come back down, I want you to be best friends again.'

My heart sank. I felt my only chance of getting back with Yasmin was if her mum organised it. I didn't think we could do it on our own.

When we got up to Yasmin's room, she collected a pair of jeans and a sweatshirt and walked coldly out into the bathroom. Normally she'd change in front of me, no problem. In fact, we're having a bit of competition over our vests. Yasmin's way out in the lead with a pink spotty crop top with sparkly straps. I don't have any crop tops. It'll be bad enough having to wear a bra when the time comes. I stick to my good old vests. My favourite is green and stripey.

While Yasmin was in the bathroom, I sat down on her bed. I felt a bit shaky. But when I heard the bathroom door open, I jumped up again. That's how bad things were. I didn't even dare to sit on her bed.

Yasmin came back in and hung her school uniform in the wardrobe. Her room's always tidy compared to mine. Watching her put her things away, I decided that being tidy was kind of easier when you're angry.

She slammed the wardrobe door shut and went back downstairs. I felt nervous. She hadn't said a single word to me! I followed her downstairs. She waited for me just outside the kitchen door, but she didn't look at me. We entered the kitchen together. Her mum looked up and beamed.

'Friends again?' she asked. Yasmin nodded. I shook my head. Mrs Saffet looked a bit stressy.

'Look, we can't sit down and have a lovely jolly tea with you in the middle of a row,' she said. 'What's this all about anyway?'

'It was nothing,' I said quickly. 'I can't even remember how it started.'

'I can remember,' said Yasmin. 'You called me stupid. Last night on the phone.' Suddenly I lost my rag. I was sick of all this.

'Well, you *are* stupid!' I burst out. Whoops, I had to be careful here. I had to control myself. 'You're stupid, I'm stupid, everybody's stupid. Aren't they?' I looked at Mrs Saffet for support.

'I'm certainly stupid, Ruby!' she laughed. 'I put Zerrin's red T-shirt in the wash today with some whites and now Yasmin's dad has pink underpants! What's the most stupid thing you've ever done?'

'Well, the most stupid thing . . .' I hesitated. I had to think of something really bizarre. I had to make Yasmin laugh. 'I tried to eat a giraffe once, but I started at the wrong end.'

Yasmin laughed! A big snort of laughter burst out of her. She hadn't meant to. She'd *had* to.

'The stupidest thing I ever did,' Yasmin said suddenly, 'was trying to steal an elephant from the zoo. I tried to fold it up but it wouldn't fit in my bag!'

I got the helpless giggles. I would have laughed at anything Yasmin said, because it was such a relief.

Mrs Saffet looked satisfied and started messing about with the tea things. Yasmin smiled at me – a proper, friendly smile.

'Sorry I was horrid, Ruby,' she said. 'I was only in a stress with you because I hated the way Hannah copied everything I did.'

'She only copies you because you're such a legend,' I told her. 'What with your pink socks and your crop tops and your hair that's ten metres long!'

'Twenty metres, you mean!' Yas grinned. 'I'm going to have to get a team of little boys to follow me around, holding it up like a train!'

'We should ring Hannah after tea,' I said, 'and make sure you two are friends again in time for the sleepover tomorrow.'

'Have you had a row with Hannah too?' asked Yasmin's mum, shaking her head in a mock hopeless way.

'Yasmin's so good at it, though,' I said, still trying to keep everything light and funny. 'It's a shame we can't have an arguments lesson at school. She'd be top of the class. She'd be in the Olympic arguing team.'

We then launched into an amazing imitation of the Olympic arguing event, with Yasmin arguing in English for Great Britain and me arguing in Chinese. I don't actually speak Chinese but I can make the right kind of sounds.

'OK, OK, that's enough!' laughed Mrs Saffet, carrying a wonderful lemon drizzle cake to the table.

'OK,' I said. 'You win. Or is that my Chinese teammate Yu Win?'

Another storm of helpless giggling. We were getting hysterical. We had to calm down now, because if you laugh too much you start feeling sick, and you certainly can't get stuck into a yummy tea if your tummy's feeling funny.

We had the most fantastic tea. It was all the more amazing because we'd had such a horrid grumpy day. I was *never* going to have a row with Yasmin ever again. We were going to be best friends for ever, no matter what.

After tea we watched a *Shrek* DVD. I so adore those films. I don't know who I love best: Donkey or Puss in Boots. I could watch them all day. It was quite a noisy movie, so when the phone rang we could hardly hear it.

'Leave it,' said Yasmin. 'Mum'll pick up in the kitchen. Hey, Ruby – I've had a brilliant idea!' She turned to me with a huge, dazzling grin. 'Why don't you stay the night with us? Then we can spend all day together tomorrow, and we can go over to your house about lunchtime and get everything ready for the sleepover!'

I froze. This was impossible. I had to go to Froggo's barbecue tomorrow at twelve, and

Yasmin was going to be livid when she found out she wasn't invited. Before I even had a moment to answer, though, Mrs Saffet came in.

'Turn that thing off for a minute, Yasmin!' she said. She sounded a bit tense. Yasmin paused the DVD. 'Ruby, your brother Joe is on the phone. He's been frantic with worry. We really should have phoned him to tell him where you were.'

I felt my face go bright red, then drain away to ghastly white. Joe! I hadn't called Joe! He'd been frantic! A horrid cold feeling spread through my tummy, as if I'd swallowed a frozen snake.

'Just have a word with him, Ruby,' said Mrs Saffet, pointing to the phone on the coffee table.

My hand was shaking.

'Hello . . . Joe?' I said. 'I'm so, so sorry I didn't ring you . . .'

'I want you back here in ten minutes,' growled Joe menacingly. 'You are dead meat.'

CHAPTER 11
It's touch and go

MRS SAFFET drove me back home right away. I felt sick with dread and guilt. Why hadn't I thought of phoning Joe? Who'd have thought he'd get all worried, just like a parent? And why did life have to be a series of blood-curdling rows? I'd only just made it up with Yasmin, and now Joe was going to eat me alive.

'So, Ruby – I'll come over to your house tomorrow morning, OK?' whispered Yasmin. Omigawd!! When I said I'd make it up with Yasmin, I may have been speaking too soon. I turned to her and grabbed her hand. Not that she was going to run away, obviously – her mum was doing forty miles per hour down the bypass.

'Listen, Yas,' I said – loudly, because I needed her mum to overhear and be on my side. 'Why don't you come over later tomorrow – because there's something I've got to do before the sleep-over.'

'What?' demanded Yasmin – rather rudely, but it still made me cringe.

Briefly my mind whizzed through a thousand stupid lies I could have told, but I was sort of sick of lies. Somehow you always get found out and made to look a total plonker.

'I have to go to Froggo's barbecue,' I said. 'It's a lunchtime thing. It'll be over by four.'

Yasmin stared at me. Her eyes looked big and her face went red. She was certainly angry.

'You never told me you were going to Froggo's barbecue!' she said accusingly.

'Er – possibly because you weren't speaking to me, remember?'

'I only wasn't speaking to you today!' snapped Yasmin. 'You could have told me yesterday!'

I knew she was jealous that Froggo hadn't invited her, but she was sort of using her jealousy to give me grief about not *telling* her about it, for goodness' sake.

'Yas, listen!' I raised my voice. 'Froggo told me not to tell anybody because he hadn't been allowed to invite Max, and he was afraid Max would find out if I told anybody!'

'I would never have told Max!' retorted Yasmin. 'I wouldn't have breathed a word to anybody!'

'Yasmin, Yasmin!' called her mum over her shoulder. 'Do give it a rest! You're so exhausting sometimes! Just like your dad. OK, Ruby – do give my apologies to Joe.'

We had reached my house. I thanked Mrs Saffet for the lift, jumped out, picked up my things, and turned back to Yas.

'See you around six, then!' I trilled, as if everything was totally cool between us.

Yas nodded grumpily. I had to rely on her mum to bring her round.

'And don't forget to ring Hannah and make it up with her!' I added, just before slamming the door. Then I turned and ran up my front path. Out of the frying pan into the fire.

While I was still scrabbling in my pockets for my key, the door opened. I flinched. But it was only Tiffany. Although normally I just get irritat-

ed at having Tiffany around, this time I was quite glad to see her. Maybe I could quickly become her best little friend and she'd protect me from Joe's fury.

'Hi, Tiffany!' I said, managing to squeeze out a big smile. 'You look fantastic! Great top!'

'Ruby! Thank God you're OK!' Tiffany glanced over her shoulder upstairs. I guessed Joe was up there. Loud music was on. 'He was totally frantic!' Tiffany whispered. 'He went out and walked up and down the streets for ages! He walked all the way back to your school to see if there was an after-school club on or something! He was on the point of ringing the police when I suddenly thought of checking if you were with Yasmin.'

'But why did he get in such a stress?' I asked. 'He

often doesn't get home until six or whatever. He goes to the Dolphin Cafe or something. I never thought he'd be like this.'

'He feels he's in charge of you and he takes it seriously!' said Tiffany. 'He made you some tea. Look.'

We went into the kitchen. The table was laid for tea. Two plates, two mugs, some bread and butter, cheese, and beans on toast – stone cold and untouched. It was a boyish sort of meal. Somehow it touched my heart and a tear rolled down my nose.

'Shall I go up and apologise to him?' I croaked. 'Or is he too cross?'

'Let him cool down up there for a bit,' said Tiffany. 'I'll tell him you're home. Don't worry, I don't think he'll hit you or anything. Joe hates rows.'

Tiffany was being very kind to me. But a horrid little spear of resentment went through me now. Who did she think she was, telling me what Joe was like? I'd lived with Joe for ten years. I'd rowed with him almost non-stop for a decade. She'd just turned up on our sofa in the past few months, but already she acted as if Joe was her property and I was some kind of random stranger who'd only met him once in the street or something.

'I'm watching *The Simpsons*,' she said. 'Come on, Ruby. That'll cheer you up.'

'I won't be a minute,' I said. Tears were still trying to squeeze themselves out of my eyes. 'It's OK, you go and watch *The Simpsons*. I'll be OK.'

Tiffany went off right away, looking relieved. Anybody would rather watch *The Simpsons* than comfort a crying child, of course. Especially Tiffany.

I stared at the ghostly tea-table for a minute. Obviously I couldn't eat the beans on toast, because I'd just had a huge tea at Yasmin's. But maybe we could microwave them for breakfast or something. I managed to find room for them in the fridge. I stacked the slices of bread and butter neatly and put them in a plastic box in the fridge too.

I cleared the rest of the table and wiped it down, even though there weren't any crumbs. I remembered earlier when I'd watched Yasmin hanging up her school clothes. It's easier to be tidy if you're angry. It's easier to be tidy if you're sad too. You want to be doing something that's nothing to do with your problem. And once you've tidied things, they do look nice, even I have to admit that.

Now I was going to tiptoe upstairs to my total tip of a room and creep into my tree house. I didn't really want to sit and watch *The Simpsons* with Tiffany. I didn't like the way she talked about Joe as if he was *hers* or something.

Just as I reached the landing, Joe's door flew open. He stood there glaring at me. There was a hole in his sock. I nearly laughed. Not that it was a joke, not that I felt remotely like laughing, just that it was such a serious moment – so *not* the moment to even smile.

'I'm really sorry, Joe,' I said. 'I didn't think you'd be worried.'

'You don't think,' he snarled. 'That's your trouble. You're brainless.'

'I'm really sorry,' I said softly. Another tear ran down my nose.

Joe went on glaring, but he didn't pull my hair or give me a Chinese burn or anything. Suddenly I remembered something.

'How's Auntie Megan?' I asked, feeling really guilty that I hadn't given her a thought for the past two hours. If she died, it would be my fault.

'It's touch and go,' he said.

I felt sick and sad and terrified.

Suddenly the phone rang. There's a phone in Mum and Dad's bedroom, on their bedside table. We both rushed in there, but it stopped ringing before we got to it. Tiffany had picked up downstairs. I hated her again immediately. How dare she pick up the phone in our house when there were two of us at home?

Joe picked it up anyway. I was dreading bad news about Auntie Megan. My legs almost gave way and I sat on the bed.

'Hello?' said Joe. 'I'm on the upstairs phone, you can hang up now.'

He listened for a minute. A weird little frown came across his brow. It wasn't an *Auntie-has-died* frown, it was smaller than that. More kind of irritated. And to do with me.

'She's here,' he said, looking at me and sounding a bit like a policeman who had me under arrest. 'Just one moment.'

He covered up the mouthpiece for a moment before handing the phone to me.

'Somebody called Lauren,' he snapped, 'asking if the sleepover's still on tomorrow. You can forget about that for one thing.' Then he handed the phone over to me and marched out.

'Hi,' I said weakly.

'Oh, Ruby!' I heard Lauren's excited voice. 'Is the sleepover still on? Did you make it up with Yasmin? Are she and Hannah friends again? My mum wants to know, because we've done all this baking – the sleepover's still on, isn't it?'

CHAPTER 12
What? What? What?

'YES,' I SAID. My voice came out like a tiny croak, as if I was a very young toad.

'What's wrong?' asked Lauren. 'You sound as if you've been crying.'

'I'm just in the middle of a row with Joe,' I said.

Lauren laughed. *Laughed!* It's funny how sometimes, in a split second, you can hate one of your very best friends.

'Oh, boys are awful, aren't they?' she said in a gossipy way. 'You should see the rows I have with Alfie!'

Honestly! How could she compare Joe with Alfie? Alfie's tiny. He's in Year One, for goodness sake. A row with Alfie? It would be like having a row with a teddy bear.

I promised her that the sleepover was still on, crossing my fingers secretly for luck, and told her to come tomorrow at six. That would leave me two hours to get everything ready. Although I still wasn't sure exactly what there was to get ready. I felt a stab of panic. How on earth did you actually organise a sleepover?

Moments later, when I'd finished talking to Lauren, I decided to go downstairs again. Although Tiffany was one of my least favourite people in the world, she was the only person actually in the house right now who would be even remotely on my side. I tiptoed past Joe's bedroom door and went down.

Tiffany was still watching *The Simpsons*. In fact, she was in hysterics. I sat down beside her and tried to tune in to it. I do adore *The Simpsons*, but right now I couldn't focus on anything except how to make sure Joe didn't cancel my sleepover. Tiffany was my only hope. But how did I get her on my side?

'Ha, ha, ah, ah!' cackled Tiffany, thumping the

cushions and gasping. It wasn't the ideal moment to raise the tricky subject of organising a party. I waited while Tiffany recovered from her giggling fit. She blew her nose on a tissue and wiped her eyes.

At last the episode ended. Thank goodness! I now had a few moments while the ads were on to broach the subject.

'Tiffany,' I said, 'I'm having a sleepover tomorrow night.'

'Oh, fab, Ruby. Hope you enjoy it,' said Tiffany, picking up *Heat* magazine. She wasn't really listening.

'The thing is,' I went on, 'just now, when I was upstairs with Joe, he said I could forget the whole idea.'

'Oh, don't take any notice of him,' said Tiffany, looking at some pictures of celebs with stains on their clothes.

'Please, Tiffany, can you ask him to let me have the sleepover?' I begged.

Tiffany finally clocked my desperate tone and turned away from the magazine. She looked at me in a slightly muddled way.

'What?' she asked. 'What were you saying, Ruby, sorry?'

'I was going to have a sleepover tomorrow night,' I said. 'It's only Yasmin and Lauren and Hannah and me. It's all organised and everything. They're all bringing food and stuff. Only I'm afraid Joe is going to stop me having it.'

Tiffany smiled and patted my hand reassuringly. 'Oh, don't worry about him,' she said. 'Of course he won't stop you! – Wait!' Suddenly a look of horror crossed her face.

'What?' I gasped. 'What? What?'

'We're going to a party tomorrow night!' she said. 'Oh no – your mum and dad won't be here, will they? Oh God! We'll have to find you a babysitter! I know! I'll ring Holly!'

Tiffany knows Holly slightly from school. What she doesn't know is that Holly can't stand her. Not that Holly makes a big thing about it. I've just seen the way she reacts when Tiffany's name is mentioned. She's got a sarcastic little curl of the lip which is really stylish. I've been practising it in secret.

'What's her number?' asked Tiffany. I froze. Tiffany mustn't ring Holly! As if she was my mum or something! Holly would never, *never* agree to babysit for me if Tiffany asked her.

'It's on my mobile!' I said. 'I'll call her.'

90

I raced into the kitchen and ransacked my schoolbag. Tiffany had followed me in and was watching anxiously. Of course, if we couldn't get a babysitter, her night out with Joe would be ruined. I couldn't find my phone. My hands were shaking. Where was the stupid thing?

'I can't find it!' I yelled. 'Wait! Her landline number is on the fridge!' Tiffany grabbed our phone. 'It's all right, I'll talk to her!' I gabbled desperately.

'No, no, Ruby, relax, it's fine,' said Tiffany, dialling Holly's number. It was so *not* fine.

'Oh hi,' she said, smiling a kind of plastic smile into the phone. 'Is Holly there? This is Tiffany . . . Well, me and Joe were wondering if Holly could

babysit for Ruby tomorrow night because we've got to go out and her parents are away.'

Tiffany listened for a bit, and a little frown line appeared between her eyebrows.

'OK, then. Sorry to bother you. Bye!' She hung up. She sounded disappointed.

'That was her mum,' she said. 'Holly's just had a couple of wisdom teeth out. So she's not well enough, apparently.' She made little speech marks in the air around the words 'not well enough'. How horrid of her not to feel sorry for Holly! I hope Tiffany has to have her wisdom teeth out one day – in public, without any painkillers.

'Who else could we ask?' Tiffany tapped her fingers on the side of the fridge. She opened the fridge door, got out a can of Coke and cracked it open. She should have asked me first. That was my family's Coke. 'Jess will be at the party, or I'd ask her. Jeez, Ruby, why do you have to be such a little kid? Maybe we could leave you on your own? Knowing our luck, though, you'd burn the house down . . . Hmmm.'

I was speechless. She just saw me as a nuisance. And if I burnt the house down, that would just be inconvenient for her, rather than a major tragedy for our whole family – maybe even our whole street.

92

At this point we heard Joe coming downstairs.

'Houston, we have a problem,' Tiffany told him. 'I can't get a babysitter for Ruby tomorrow, because everybody we know is going to be at the Midsummer Rave.'

She opened the fridge again, took out another can of Coke, opened it and handed it to Joe.

'No, thanks,' he said. Tiffany glared in surprise. 'You never *ask*,' he snapped, in an irritated voice. Then he said something really amazing.

'There's no need to get a babysitter anyway.' He walked off down the kitchen with his back to us, and got a mug out of the china cupboard. Then he turned round and stared at Tiffany in a challenging kind of way. 'Because I'm going to stay at home and look after Ruby.'

'Whaaaaaaaat?!' screamed Tiffany.

I backed off towards the door. This was going to be dangerous.

CHAPTER 13
I can't wait!

THERE WAS A shouting match. Tiffany was doing most of the shouting. I raced upstairs to my bedroom and hid in my tree house. Soon I heard the front door slam. Good! Tiffany had gone. Then I heard Joe's footsteps thundering up the stairs. I cringed, but he went past my door and into his room. Then his door slammed. All this slamming!

Loud music broke out — a sign that Joe was not to be disturbed. I suddenly realised I needed to tidy my room. After all, I was having a sleepover tomorrow night. I climbed down my tree-house rope ladder and started to pick up all the bits and pieces I'd chucked on the floor.

Then I heard it: a faint, faraway buzz. The sound of my phone when switched to vibrate. But where was it? Where? Where? And who was calling? Yasmin reporting another row with Hannah? Desperately I tried to locate the sound. It was coming from my door. My blazer was hanging up there – the phone was in the pocket! I grabbed it. The display said *HOLLY*.

'Holly!' I yelled. 'How are you? How are you feeling?'

'Lithen,' said Holly. 'I thound a bit thrange becauthe of my teeth. I can't open my mouth properly. But my mum thaid you need a babythitter tomorrow and I'm thure I'll feel better by then.'

'Oh, it's OK.' I realised I didn't really need a babysitter if Joe was going to stay in. 'Not if you're feeling bad.'

'I don't want to go to the Midthummer Rave,' confessed Holly, 'becauthe my fathe haath thwelled up. I look like a chipmunk! Lithen – I'd much rather thpend the evening with you.'

'I'm having a sleepover, though, remember?' I

reminded her. 'With Lauren and Yasmin and Hannah. And Mum and Dad are away.'

'Oh yeth! Tho you are! How lovely!' said Holly. 'I can thtay the night, no problem.'

'Fantastic!' I was so overjoyed at the thought of Holly staying over, I didn't tell her Joe would be there anyway. I didn't feel too guilty about it, either. First, Joe might *really* want to go to the Midsummer Rave, and if Holly was looking after us, he'd be able to. I'd caused him enough grief already today. Second (and more sneaky), I was still hoping that Holly and Joe would get together one day and I thought it would be a great chance for them to spend some quality time together.

'There'th juth one thing,' said Holly. 'You've got to promithe to wear thome thpecial thingth that I'll bring.'

'OK, I promise!' I assured her. 'I'll wear any special thing. As long as it's not a pink frilly frock!' I love mysteries. Already Holly had brought some extra excitement into my plans. I thanked her and we arranged that she'd come tomorrow at five, in case anything needed organising.

After that I went on tidying my room. I felt better already. For the first time I was starting to look forward to my sleepover. It was going to be great!

My phone buzzed again. Oh no! Somebody was going to cancel! I picked up. The display flashed *FROGGO*. No way! Was he going to cancel?

'Bring a swimsuit tomorrow,' said Froggo. 'We've got an inflatable pool.'

'Wow!' I screamed. 'Mega!' I couldn't wait for tomorrow. As my parents were away, Froggo said his mum would pick me up around twelve.

Now all I had to do was find my swimsuit. I hadn't used it since our trip at Whitsun, when my dad had tried to teach me to swim. It smelled faintly of swimming pools from the time Mum and Deb and I had been to the spa. We'd forgotten to wash it! Never mind.

Next day was brilliantly sunny. Joe normally lies in bed till noon, but this time he got up and cooked a fabulous breakfast of scrambled eggs with cheese. He seemed to be in a good mood. Maybe he was secretly relieved to have got rid of Tiffany, although their relationship has been on and off and on and off ever since it started. I hoped this time it would *really* be over.

'Joe,' I said nervously, 'I'm sorry, but I can't cancel this sleepover because Lauren's mum has made loads of cakes for it, and if I cancel it, Lauren will never stop crying and –

'Enough!' snapped Joe.

My heart thudded. But it was only a pretend snap.

'OK, I'll endure the torture of your goddam sleepover,' he sighed. 'You'll have to make it up to me, though.'

'Anything!' I cried desperately. 'I'll do anything!'

'OK,' said Joe. 'Promise that you will be my slave for ever, and write my thank-you letters at Christmas, and look after me when I get old and cook me pies and mop up my drool.'

'I promise!' I yelled excitedly.

'OK,' said Joe wearily, putting his hands in his pockets and slouching against the fridge.

'What do you need for this sleepover nightmare?' he asked. 'Boxes of matches, obviously – petrol, knives, that sort of thing?'

I laughed. Joe must be feeling better if he was joking again. I told him we didn't need anything because the others were bringing the food. I didn't tell him Holly was coming because I thought it would be fun to surprise him. And if he knew she was coming, he might pretend he had to go out. He seems extra shy of her sometimes.

Froggo's barbecue was a blast. We had the best time, attacking one another with the hose and splashing in the pool.

'It's not wasting water,' explained Froggo's mum, 'because we're going to use it to water the garden afterwards.' Froggo's family are eco-warriors. They're so cool.

The barbecue was delicious, and we ate in the shadow of a big tree. Froggo hasn't got a tree house, though — even though the tree would be perfect. It's such a waste.

The Froggos delivered me home at four o'clock on the dot. Joe was watching TV but he switched it off when I arrived.

'Mum rang,' he said. 'Auntie Megan is hanging on. They think she'll probably make it.'

'Hoorah!' I screamed. 'Brilliant, brilliant, brilliant!' I jumped up and down on the spot. Then I dived down on to Joe (who was still sprawled on the sofa) and we had a friendly fight. Sometimes we do still have a cuddle while we're watching a scary movie.

'I bought a couple of five-star luxury pizzas,' said Joe. 'Squashed Beetle flavour. I thought you ought to offer these sleepover girls *something*, for God's sake. And various types of juice.'

'Oh thanks, Joe!' I screamed in delight and gave him a massive hug.

'Local Sixth Former Suffocated by Sister in Freak Attack,' he gasped in his newspaper headline voice. I jumped up. There was still stuff to do.

First I had to admire Joe's pizzas. Then I had a quick bath because I was a bit muddy from Froggo's pool and garden. Then, because it was supposed to be a Midsummer's Night Celtic thing, I put on my special black T-shirt, which has stars and a moon which glow in the dark. My shorts were just ordinary, though. I didn't want to wear a skirt made from the skin of ancient donkeys or anything. There was no need to be *that* Celtic.

The front doorbell rang. I raced downstairs and met Joe coming up, an expression of mock terror on his face.

'You answer the door!' he hissed. 'I can't face a crowd of your evil friends! I'll be in my room if you need me.'

It wasn't an evil friend, of course. It was Holly. And she was wearing a mask – the face of a smiley Cheshire cat.

'Ruby, you legend!' She hugged me. 'I can talk properly now. My mouth doesn't hurt nearly so much today. But my face is still puffed up so I'm wearing this mask. And you've got to wear one, too, to make me feel at ease.'

As she stepped inside, she handed me a carrier bag full of masks. Wonderful! There was a rat, a hippo, a pirate and Spiderman, and a bear and a tiger and a cow.

'There's a monkey in there somewhere,' she said.

I found it and put it on. While I was fiddling with the elastic band, I saw Holly look up. Joe was standing on the landing.

'Oh, hi,' he said, trying to sound cool.

'I asked Holly to babysit in case you wanted to go to the Midsummer Rave,' I explained.

Joe pulled a face.

'I don't think I'll bother,' he said. 'I've got to finish a project this weekend.'

'If you come down and join us sometime,' I said, 'you'll have to wear a mask.'

I grabbed the Spiderman mask and ran upstairs with it. I held it out to Joe. He shrugged again.

'Why wait till then?' he said, and put it on. Then he went back into his room.

Holly laughed rather nervously below.

'I've bought a few little things,' she said. 'I assume we'll have a picnic tea in the garden?'

I squealed with delight. I hadn't thought that far ahead. A picnic! Oh yes! That had been the plan.

We laid a cloth on the lawn, and Holly had brought little paper lanterns, which we dotted about among the flower beds.

'They can have candles in them,' she said. 'We'll light them when it gets really dark, which won't be until about ten o'clock, of course.'

'Oh great!' I grinned. 'Yasmin wanted to have a bonfire but my dad said no. He composts everything instead.'

'Hmmm,' said Holly. 'Correct, of course, in environmental terms, but we can hardly sit around the compost heap singing songs. Just as well I brought the candles.'

'Mum doesn't let us light candles indoors,' I said. 'But I'm sure it'll be OK out here.'

'Don't worry, Ruby,' said Holly in a pompous headmistressy voice. 'I'm in charge and I won't allow any silliness. Nobody's going to burn down the town – not without my permission anyway.'

Holly had also brought some balloons and a pump, and soon we had tied lovely bunches of balloons to the garden shed and the fence and the runner bean canes. The balloons danced in the breeze. It looked absolutely magic.

Yasmin and Hannah and Lauren arrived, all bringing loads of amazing food. When they saw the garden they screamed in delight.

'Could you keep the noise down, please, or I'll have to call the police!' came a sudden bossy voice.

For a split second my blood ran cold. But it was only Joe looking down from his bedroom window – still wearing his Spiderman mask.

Yasmin had chosen the tiger one, Hannah had gone for the pirate and Lauren had chosen the cow.

'OK,' said Holly. 'I'll go and put the pizzas on.' She went indoors.

'I can't wait for it to get dark!' said Yasmin. 'Once the candles are all lit, we can make a wish. But it has to stay secret.'

·I knew what mine would be. It would be so tempting to wish that Joe and Holly would get together. But there were more important things to think about. My wish would be about Auntie Megan. She needed all the magic help she could get.

Everyone sat down around the picnic cloth and started talking about Yasmin's shoes. She was wearing gold metallic square-toe pumps. They were just the sort of thing a Celtic priestess would wear nowadays. Suddenly I thought I ought to go in and help Holly.

I heard voices in the kitchen. Spiderman was in there. They were talking about some random teenage thing – the WOMAD world music festival or something.

'Do you need any help, Holly?' I asked. Just then the front doorbell rang.

'I'll answer it!' I yelled. Holly and Joe stayed right where they were. They assumed it was another of my guests, I suppose. I went to the door and peeped through the spyhole. Omigawd! It was Tiffany!

I ran back to the kitchen, desperately making *sshhh!* signs. 'It's Tiffany!' I hissed.

Joe shrugged. I couldn't see his face because of the Spiderman mask.

'Tell her I'm out,' he said.

I went back to the door. My legs were shaking slightly. What if she burst in and found Spiderman and Hollycat together? It would set her off on one of her yelling fits and it would ruin my party. I took a deep breath, removed my mask, gathered all my available courage and opened the door.

'Joe says he's out,' I stammered. Oh no! What an idiot! Why on earth had I said that?

Tiffany blushed and looked insulted.

'I don't want to see him anyway,' she said in a proud, angry voice. 'I just brought back various bits of his junk he'd left at my house.' She handed me the carrier bag and marched off down the path.

Hastily I nipped back inside and shut the door. Wow! This must be it, then. I went back into the kitchen.

'Stuff you left at her house,' I said, handing the bag over to Joe. He didn't even look inside. He just tossed it in a corner.

'I think the pizza's ready now,' said Holly. 'Can you pour out the juice, Joe? Ruby, bring some paper napkins – over there.'

The most delicious smell was spreading through the kitchen.

As we walked out, carrying the pizza and juice and stuff, Hannah and Yasmin and Lauren all burst out clapping and cheering. I'd been dreading this party and now it was shaping up to be the best ever.

Holly cut the pizza up and passed it round. Everybody had some, in spite of their foodie fads.

'When can we do the spells?' asked Yasmin.

'When it's dark,' said Holly. 'You'll have to be patient.'

'I've got a spell you do with mirrors,' said Yasmin. 'If it works, you see your future husband looking over your shoulder. In the dark. In the mirror.'

'What if he's a fat, bald, smelly old nerd?' asked Hannah.

'I don't suppose any of us will be *that* lucky!' laughed Holly. We all cracked up.

'While we're waiting for it to get dark,' said Hannah, 'can we play games?'

'Oh yes!' said Holly. 'I've got loads. Funny ones and creepy ones.'

The sun was sinking slowly down the sky, bathing the back wall of our house in golden light. A few birds were singing softly in the hedge.

'This is the best party ever!' said Lauren, clapping her hands in delight.

'Yes,' said Holly. 'We should drink a toast to Ruby. We owe it all to her. She had a dream, a vision, a plan: she wanted to have a sleepover and she stuck to her guns through thick and thin. It just goes to show what you can achieve if you have guts and determination. To Ruby!'

Everybody raised their cups and said, 'To Ruby!'

I stared at my shoes, feeling embarrassed. It was nice what Holly had said, but it was garbage. The sleepover wasn't my plan. It had been forced on me by Yasmin. Right from the start I'd been nervous about it. I'd almost managed to cancel it at one stage. I'd dreaded it, and trying to plan it had wound me up in so many tangles. I'd hated the very thought of it at times.

It seemed as if the sleepover had almost happened by itself, but that I had got the credit for it. Holly had said I had guts and determination. But the truth was I'd been cowardly and useless – as usual.

Oh well. Nobody seemed to have noticed. So maybe I had got away with it.

Don't miss Ruby in her next
brilliant misadventure:

Ruby Rogers
Get Me Out of Here!

Available now